Building a Case

by Nomi J. Waldman

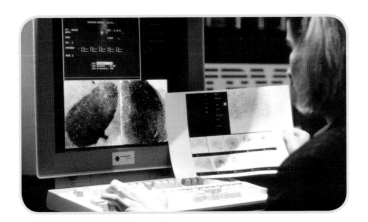

Strategy Focus

As you read, **monitor** how well you understand what is happening. Reread to **clarify** parts that seem unclear.

 HOUGHTON MIFFLIN   BOSTON

Key Vocabulary

case a problem or event that is being looked into

clue hint; a piece of information that helps solve a mystery

criminal a person who has committed a crime

detective a person who tries to solve a crime

evidence facts or signs that show the truth

solution the answer to a mystery

suspect a person who might be guilty of a crime

suspense worry or uncertainty about what will happen

witness a person who sees or hears something

Word Teaser

I can carry a musical instrument. I am also a crime that the police are trying to solve. What am I?

The police get a phone call. Someone robbed
a store at the corner of Elm Street and Main
Street! Money is missing from the cash register.

Crimes like this happen every day. Every crime the police work on is called a case. It will take a team of detectives to solve the case of the store robbery.

Floor Plan

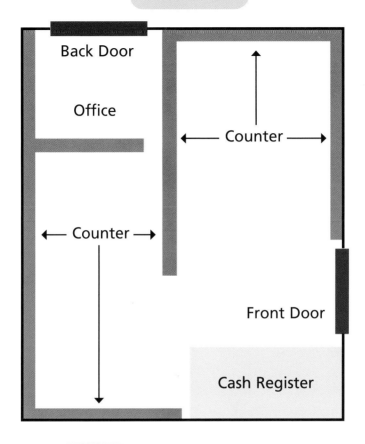

First, the team heads to the scene of the crime. One detective makes a floor plan of the store. Another takes pictures. Others write down what they see. This will help the team remember everything.

The detectives have many questions.
When did the robbery happen? Did just one
criminal rob the store, or was more than one
person involved? How did the robbers get in?

They study fingerprints. They compare them to fingerprints from other crime scenes. They look for a match. A match might help them figure out who robbed the store.

Some witnesses think they saw the
criminal. A police artist listens to what they
say. Then the artist draws a picture. Maybe
someone will know whose picture it is.

The case is beginning to make sense. The detectives think they know who committed the robbery. They ask all the police in town to help them find this suspect.

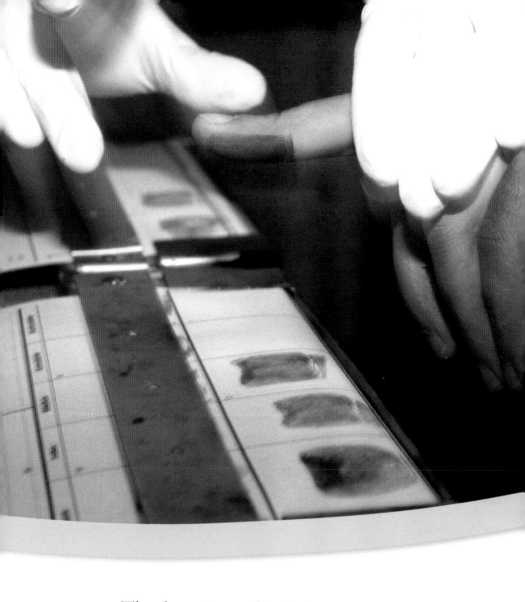

The detectives will ask the suspect
questions. They will check the suspect's
fingerprints. They will ask the witnesses if
they think this is the criminal.

There's a lot of suspense until the crime is solved. The detectives must get answers to all their questions.

The police have all the evidence they need. They are ready to arrest the suspect. Soon the detectives hope to say, "Case closed!"

Putting Words to Work

1. Complete this sentence, using your own words and the word **clue**.
   The **detective** looked carefully at the crime scene because _____.

2. Why must the **solution** to the case make sense?

3. Why might one **witness** be more helpful than another?

4. How can **evidence** help a **detective**?

5. PARTNER ACTIVITY: Think of a word you learned in the book. Explain its meaning to your partner and give an example.

Answer to Word Teaser
a case